FELIZ NEW YEAR, AVA GABRIELA!

Alexandra Alessandri

illustrated by
Addy Rivera Sonda

Albert Whitman & Company
Chicago, Illinois

The day before New Year's Eve, Ava Gabriela stood with Mamá and Papá in Abuelita's finca. Ava's tías and tíos, primas and primos didn't feel like familia yet. They felt like strangers.

"Say hola," Mamá told Ava.
Ava's heart thumped like Papá's tambor.
She opened her mouth.

Nothing.
"Speak up, Ava Gabriela," Papá said.
Abuelita added, "Mija, ¿Te comieron la lengua los ratones?"
Tío Mario's laugh thundered. Ava hid behind Mamá. No, mice had *not* nibbled her tongue! But how was she supposed to speak with so many eyes staring at her?

Ava wished she didn't feel as small as a mouse.
"It's okay," Tía Nena said. "Want to help us make buñuelos?"
Ava hesitated. But the fried cheesy fritters were her favorite.
Mamá always made them for the holidays.
When Tía Nena held out her hand...

Ava took it.
Her primos Sarita and Pedro joined them in the kitchen.
Together, they cracked eggs, measured flour, and tossed in cheese.

When the others weren't looking, she swiped some.
Ava loved cheese. "Mmm," she murmured. Maybe her
voice hadn't completely disappeared.

They mixed, squeezed, and kneaded the dough. Then Tía Nena dusted the counter with flour, and they rolled the masa into round bolitas. Her cousins chattered and laughed. Ava didn't.

But when Ava wasn't looking, Tía Nena sprinkled *her* with flour.
Ava giggled. She wanted to yell, "Food fight!" but the words stuck
on her tongue. Why couldn't they just come out?

"Done!" Tía Nena said. "Go on. Have fun."

Sarita and Pedro dashed out of the kitchen. Ava trailed behind. She wanted to call out, "Wait!" but her voice hid like a mouse in its hole.

Instead, she wandered through the finca alone.

She found Mamá with Abuelita sipping cafecitos and eating bocadillos.
"Would you like one?" Abuelita asked.
Ava nodded. She nibbled the small guava square until it was all gone.

"Why am I so shy?" she whispered.

"Oh, amor," Mamá said. "There's nothing wrong with being shy. When you're ready, your voice will come out and play."

Mamá gathered Ava in a giant hug. It made Ava feel a tiny bit better.

Ava kept exploring until she found her primo Pedro sitting cross-legged on the terrace floor, blowing up balloons. She wanted to ask, "What are you doing?" Instead, she sat quietly beside him and watched.

"Did you come to help with el Año Viejo?" Pedro asked.

She'd never heard of the Old Year.

"It's a balloon doll we build to say goodbye to the old year. At midnight, we pop him!"

Ava's mouth rounded into a perfect O. She wanted to say, "Yes! I'll help!"

Nothing.

Her too-shy voice was going to make her miss out on all the fun.

"Why don't you build the Año Viejo?" Pedro said. "I'll blow up more balloons."

Pedro puffed and Ava stuffed. Together, they built the Old Year doll until all that was left was to draw his face. Pedro handed her a marker.

Ava's heart thumped like a tambor. She should say thank you. She *could* say thank you.

"Gracias."

The word was whispery soft but tasted sweet like dulce de leche.

She drew a mouth on the doll—and giggled. It looked ready to talk like a loro mojado. Maybe soon *she* would be the one talking like a wet parrot!

The next morning, Ava awoke determined.
Everyone bustled to get the finca ready for the new year. Music filled the air.
In the kitchen, Mamá and Abuelita filled cups with grapes. Twelve grapes
for twelve months of good luck. That gave Ava an idea!

She plucked one and said a silent wish: *Please let me not be shy today.*
Everyone would eat the grapes at midnight, but she needed luck now.
Feeling brave, Ava dashed out of the kitchen.

"¡Buenos días, Ava Gabriela!" Tía Nena called.
"Good morning!" Ava called back.
"Slow down!" Pedro laughed.
Ava did, grinning. "Okay."
Her voice grew wings and hummed like a colibrí.

Except, just then, Tío Mario and Papá passed by carrying furniture.
"What are you up to, little mouse?" Tío Mario boomed. Ava squeaked.
She didn't hide, but her words stayed stuck in her throat.
What if her shyness never went away?

"Ava Gabriela," Mamá called. "Time to change!"

In her room, Ava found the clothes Mamá had laid out, including yellow underwear for good luck. Ava needed all the luck they could give her.

Outside, the lanterns on the terrace winked. Glasses clinked. Cousins shouted. Her family chattered around a table bursting with food. Tamales. Pernil. Buñuelos. Natilla.

Ava sat beside the Año Viejo. *Don't you want to play?* it seemed to ask.
She really did.

Suddenly, fireworks swished and squealed and boomed above her.
Ava dashed out onto the cool grass. She bounced on her toes and
reached her hands toward the sky.

One by one, her cousins joined her.

"Do you want to play tag?" Pedro asked.

Ava could say yes. She would say yes. With her heart galloping, Ava blurted, "Sí."

Her cousins cheered. Sarita took her hand, and together, they raced across the field. Ava felt like a mouse who'd just discovered a cupboard full of cheese. ¡Feliz!

That night, as her tíos played tambores and guitarras, Ava danced with Tía Nena. She sang at the top of her lungs, and her familia sang with her. She even whispered, "Gracias," when Tío Mario gifted her a buñuelo.

And when the clock struck midnight, Ava popped the Año Viejo with her cousins, calling out, "¡Feliz Año Nuevo!"

Author's Note

The Christmas season, which begins on December 7 (Día de las Velitas, or Little Candles' Day) and ends on January 6 (Día de los Reyes Magos, or Three Kings' Day), is a festive one for us Colombians and for many across Latin America, the Caribbean, and our respective diasporas. This season is a time for family and celebration, and New Year's Eve, or Año Nuevo, is no different.

Each New Year's Eve, tables in Colombian homes around the world are filled with delicious foods, like buñuelos, natilla, pernil, and tamales. Music as distinct as our regions accompanies our celebrations. For some, like Ava's family, it's cumbia, vallenato, and salsa. For others, it's joropo, porro, and bambuco. Most importantly, though, we open our doors to family and friends, preparing to send off the old year and bring in the new one.

We also have many traditions and superstitions for New Year's Eve. Like Ava, we eat twelve grapes and wear yellow underwear for good luck and happiness. Sometimes, we'll walk around our street at the stroke of midnight, luggage in hand, to ensure we travel well in the new year. Often, we'll clean the house to make sure all the dirt and negativity of the old year stays behind.

But perhaps the tradition I cherish most is that of el Año Viejo. This life-size doll made its way into every single one of my family's New Year's Eve celebrations—even in the United States, thousands of miles away from our Colombia. The Año Viejo represents everything we want to leave behind: disappointments, sadness, troubles. Sometimes, the adults in my family made this doll out of straw or newspaper and burned it at midnight. In recent years, we started making him out of balloons, so children could enjoy popping the Old Year goodbye.

Traditions evolve over time and place, but the heart of our celebrations has always remained the same: la familia.

Glossary

Abuelita—grandma, from Abuela, or grandmother

amor—love, a term of endearment often used in Spanish-speaking countries

bocadillo—dessert made of guava pulp and sugar, sometimes cut into squares and wrapped in dried corn leaves

bolitas—small spheres

¡Buenos días!—Good morning!

buñuelos—a staple of the Christmas season in Colombia, these fried fritters are uniformly round and made of yucca flour, cheese, and eggs

cafecitos—small coffees

colibrí—hummingbird

dulce de leche—caramel spread

El Año Viejo—the Old Year, a doll (or scarecrow) that is made to represent the old year

familia—family

¡Feliz Año Nuevo!—Happy New Year!

finca—farm

gracias—thank you

guitarras—guitars

Hablar como un loro mojado—a saying that means "to talk like a wet parrot"

Hola—Hello

Mamá—Mother

masa—dough

mija—sometimes spelled "m'ija," this is an abbreviated form of "mi hija," or "my daughter"

natilla—a traditional Colombian Christmas custard that is jellylike and made with panela (sugarcane), spices, milk, cornstarch, and vanilla

Papá—Father

pernil—roasted pork leg, often served as the main dish during the Christmas season

prima/primas—female cousin/s

primo/primos—male cousin/s

sí—yes

tamales—a dish made of a cornmeal, meat, and vegetable filling that is wrapped and boiled in banana leaves, which is often served during the Christmas season

tambor/tambores—drum/drums

¿Te comieron la lengua los ratones?—a saying that means, "Did the mice eat your tongue?"

tía/tías—aunt/aunts

tío/tíos—uncle/uncles

trompetas—trumpets

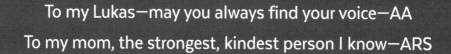

To my Lukas—may you always find your voice—AA

To my mom, the strongest, kindest person I know—ARS

Library of Congress Cataloging-in-Publication data is on file with the publisher.

Text copyright © 2020 by Alexandra Alessandri

Illustrations copyright © 2020 by Albert Whitman & Company

Illustrations by Addy Rivera Sonda

First published in the United States of America in 2020 by Albert Whitman & Company

ISBN 978-0-8075-0450-5 (hardcover)

ISBN 978-0-8075-0451-2 (ebook)

Printed in China

10 9 8 7 6 5 4 3 2 WKT 26 25 24 23 22 21

Design by Valerie Hernández

For more information about Albert Whitman & Company,
visit our website at www.albertwhitman.com.